Lodge of Perfection

**Legenda of the Lodge of Perfection**

Southern jurisdiction, U.S.A

Lodge of Perfection

**Legenda of the Lodge of Perfection**
*Southern jurisdiction, U.S.A*

ISBN/EAN: 9783337150617

Printed in Europe, USA, Canada, Australia, Japan

Cover: Foto ©Andreas Hilbeck / pixelio.de

More available books at **www.hansebooks.com**

# LEGENDA

OF THE

# LODGE OF PERFECTION.

SOUTHERN JURISDICTION, U. S. A.

CHARLESTON.

1888.

# LEGENDA, I.

---

## The Aenigma of Hiram.

# LEGENDA.

## I.

## THE ÆNIGMA OF HIRAM.

THE Divine Symbols and hieroglyphs that constitute what has in all time been called the KOSMOS, the WORLD, the UNIVERSE, or the CREATION, which is represented by the Lodge, have in all ages been misinterpreted. They are the manifestation of the Deity, the formulated expression and utterance of His THOUGHT, the unfolding and succession of the manifold in being from the Divine unity of Idea. It is of necessity that the Symbol should always be capable of being misunderstood, and, therefore, Omnipotence intended that they should be so; and these misinterpretations are the philosophies and the religions that have succeeded each other like shadows upon the water.

The Universe is an enigma, of which the Sphynx is the symbol. The whole Egyptian land was a great Book, and the teachings of this Book were repeated, translated in pictures, sculptures, architecture, in all the cities and in all the temples. The Desert itself had its eternal teachings, and its Word of Stone sat squarely upon the base of the Pyramids, before which the colossal Sphynx has meditated during so many ages, slowly burying itself in the sand. Its head, mutilated by Time, is still visible above its tomb, as if to disappear it only waited for a human voice to come and explain to the New World the problem of the Pyramids.

Superstitions, it has been said, are religious forms that survive lost ideas. All once had, as their reason of being, a truth no longer known, or a truth transfigured. Their very name, from the Latin *superstes*, signifies that which *survives*. They are the material relics of Ancient Knowledge or Opinions. Once the meaning of the Sphynx, of the Assyrian human-headed bulls and lions, of the cherubim, of the oxen under the brazen laver, of the mystic-winged and many-eyed creatures of Ezekiel, was known, at least to the Sages. Who now possesses the key to that meaning?

Nor is it only the Symbols of that first revelation which we term Creation, that are misinterpreted. The Oracles, also, have always spoken in enigmas, and whoso has not divined their meaning has, in attempting it, died. The sacred Books of the Hebrews are also Oracles—a succession of symbols and allegories—which those who read them literally the least understand. Who can interpret the Prophecies and the Apocalypse?

Masonry also has its ancient Symbols, inherited from the Mysteries and the Kabalah, and intended to veil and conceal the truth from all except the Adepts. Like the religions, also, Masonry gives false interpretations of its Symbols, to mislead those who would not value the highest philosophical truth, and the Profane to whom these interpretations may be divulged.

The Statue of Truth is always veiled. Nature reluctantly yields up to us her secrets, so that as yet we know them only in part, and imperfectly. Science is a progressive revelation, and the revelation by the written word is continuous; its true meaning, which is the revealing, being slowly evolved during the march of the centuries.

Unfortunately, the Sages die, leaving no successors, and the true interpretation of the Symbols that they used dies with them; but the false interpretations to which they resorted survive. The Symbol itself is taken for the thing or the truth symbolized. The symbolic ceremony is deemed to possess the energy of salvation; and to neglect a sacrifice or a Rite, or for any except the Priest to dare to use it, is regarded and punished as sacrilege: while dull mediocrity invents tame and common interpretations, that make the ceremony which once was solemn to be trivial, and the Symbol itself to be worthless.

But when an interpretation is in part true, and in part intentionally false or obscure, symbolism performs its own accustomed office, requiring the Initiate to separate the True from the Untrue by his own study and reflection, or to remain among the mass of those to whom the highest Truth is of the least value.

Such an interpretation is that which follows. It is given by an Adept, and, therefore, propounds the truth enigmatically, that which it plainly expresses being of less value than that which it conceals or only hints at.

"Anarchy alone flatters the prejudices of the multitude. Absolute truths are not needed for the masses; for otherwise progress would be arrested, and life would cease in humanity The ebb and flow of contrary ideas, the shock of opinions, the passions that rule the intellect, determined always by the dreams of the moment, are necessary to the intellectual growth of the peoples."

" Few men, in any age," to use the energetic language of the Oracle, "*have heard the Light speak*." The Light, indeed, in the visible world, alternates with the Shadow ; they mingle with each other, also, and the line between them is not to be defined. So also it is with Truth and Error; for Error is the shadow of the Light. Errors, also, in science and philosophy, often lead to the discovery of the truth ; and the intellect is more profitably exercised in detecting them, and so for itself extracting the gold from the ore, than in digesting the truths which those who so discovered them teach.

Let the Initiate, then, winnow the Error from the Truth in the following interpretation of a Masonic legend.

"The Grand Kabalistic Association, known in Europe under the name of MASONRY, appeared all at once in the world at the period when the Protest against the Church came to break the Christian unity. The historians of the Order do not know how to explain the origin of it. Some ascribe it to a free association of Masons, formed at the time of the building of the cathedral of Strasburg: others give it Cromwell for founder, without troubling themselves to inquire whether the rites of the English Masonry of the time of Cromwell were not organized against that chief of the Puritan anarchy; and others are ignorant enough to attribute to the Jesuits, if not the foundation, at least the continuation and direction of this society, long secret and always mysterious. Rejecting this last opinion, which refutes itself, we may reconcile the others, by saying that the Brethren-masons (*frères-maçons*) borrowed from the builders of the Cathedral of Strasburg their name and the emblems of their art; and that they were publicly organized for the first time in England, under favor of its radical institutions, and in despite of the despotism of Cromwell.

"We may add, that they have had the Templars for models, the Roses-croix for fathers, and the Johannites for ancestors. Their dogma is that of Zoroaster and Hermes; their rule is progressive initiation; their principle, equality, regulated by the hierarchy and universal fraternity: they are the continuers of the school of Alexandria, heirs of all the ancient initiations; they are the depositaries of the secrets of the Apocalypse and the Sohar; the object of their worship is Truth, represented by the Light; they tolerate all creeds, and profess but one and the same philosophy; they search for Truth alone, teach only Reality, and desire to lead all intelligences progressively to Reason.

"The allegorical object of Masonry is the rebuilding of the Temple of Solomon: its real object is the reconstitution of social unity, by the alliance of Reason and Faith; and the re-establishment of the Hierachy, in accordance with knowledge and virtue; with initiation and tests by means of degrees.

"Nothing is finer, we see, nothing grander than these ideas; but unfortunately the doctrines of unity and of sub-mission to the hierarchy have not been preserved in the uni-versal Masonry. There soon sprung up a dissident Ma-sonry, opposed to the orthodox, and the greatest calamities of the French Revolution were the consequences of this schism.

"The Freemasons have their sacred legend; that of HIRAM completed by that of CYRUS and ZOROBABEL.

"This is the legend of Hiram:

"When Solomon caused the Temple to be builded, he in-trusted his plans to an architect named HIRAM or HARAM.

"This Architect, to establish order in the work, divided the laborers according to their skill and experience: and as their number was very great, in order to be able to recognize them, whether to employ them according to their capacity, or to remunerate them according to their work, he gave to each class, to the Apprentices, Fellows, and Masters, particular pass-words and signs.

"Three Fellow-crafts who desired to usurp the rank of Mas-ter, without being entitled to it by their deserts, lay in wait at the three principal gates of the Temple, and when Hiram was about to go forth, one of them demanded of him the Masters' word, menacing him with his *Rule*.

"Hiram replied to him: '*I did not so receive the word that you demand of me.*"

"The enraged Fellow-craft struck Hiram with his *Rule of iron*, and inflicted on him the first wound.

"Hiram fled to another gate, and there found the second Fellow-craft: the same demand was made and the same reply given, and this time Hiram was struck with a *square*, or, as others say, with a *lever*.

"At the third gate was the third assassin, who finished the Master with a blow of a *mallet*.

"The three Fellow-crafts afterward hid the body under a pile of rubbish, and planted on this improvised grave a branch of *Acacia*, and then fled, like Cain after the murder of Abel.

"Meanwhile Solomon, his Architect not returning, sent nine Masters to seek him. The branch of acacia led them to find the body; they drew it from the rubbish, and as it had remained there for some days, they cried, upon raising it, *Mach-benach!* which means, 'the flesh parts from the bones.'

"The last duties were performed to Hiram, and twenty-seven Masters were then sent by Solomon to search for the murderers.

"The first was surprised in a cave; a lamp burned near him, a rivulet ran at his feet, and a poniard was near him for his defence. The Master who entered the cavern recognized the assassin, seized the poniard, and stabbed him, saying 'NEKUM!' a word that means '*Vengeance*.' His head was carried to Solomon, who was angered on seeing it, and said to him who had killed the assassin: '*Wretch! did you not know that I had reserved to myself the right to punish?*' Then all the Masters prostrated themselves, and begged for pardon for him whom his zeal had carried too far.

"The second murderer was betrayed by a man who had given him refuge. He was hidden in a grotto among the rocks, near a burning bush, over which glowed a rainbow, and a dog watched near him. The Masters eluded the vigilance of the dog, seized the criminal, bound him, and led him to Jerusalem, where he was put to death.

"The third assassin was killed by a lion, which it was necessary to conquer in order to gain possession of the body. But other versions say that the assassin defended himself against the Masters with an axe, until they succeeded in disarming him, when they took him to Solomon, who ordered him executed, to expiate his crime.

" Such is the first legend.   See now the explanation of it.

" SOLOMON is the personification of *Knowledge* and the Supreme Wisdom.

" The Temple is the realization and figure of the Holy Empire, the reign of Truth and Reason on the earth.

" Hiram is *Man* attaining Empire by means of Knowledge and Sagacity.

" He governs by Justice and Order, rewarding every one according to his works.

" Every degree of the Order has a Word which expresses its meaning.

" There is for Hiram only one Word, but this is pronounced in three different manners.

" In one manner for the Apprentices, pronounced by whom it signifies Nature, and is explained by Toil.

" In another manner for the Fellow-crafts ; and with them it means Thought, explaining itself by Study.

" In another manner for the Masters ; and in their mouth it signifies Truth, a word that is explained by Wisdom.

" This Word is that used to designate God, whose true name is ineffable and incommunicable.

" So there are three degrees in the Hierarchy, as there are three gates to the Temple.

" There are three principal rays in the Light ;

" There are three Forces in nature.

" These Forces are figured by the RULE, which unites ; the LEVER, that raises ; and the MALLET, that consolidates.

" The rebellion of the brutal instincts against the Hierarchical aristocracy of wisdom, arms itself in succession with these three forces, which it turns aside from the harmony.

" There are three typical rebels :

" The rebel against Nature ;

" The rebel against Knowledge ;

" The rebel against Truth.

"These were figured in the Hell of the ancients, by the three heads of Cerberus.

"They are figured in the Bible by Korah, Dathan, and Abiron.

"In the Masonic legend they are designated by names that vary according to the Rites.

"The first is called YUBELA and ROMVEL. He strikes the Grand Master with the *Rule*.

"It is the history of the first man put to death, in the name of the Law, by human passions.

"The second is called YUBELO or HOBHEN. He strikes Hiram with the *Lever* or the *Square*.

"So the popular Lever or the Square of a senseless Equality becomes the instrument of Tyranny in the hands of the multitude, and wounds yet more severely than the Rule the Royalty of Wisdom and Virtue.

"The third is called YUBELUM, *Abairam*, *Akhirop*, *Gibs*, or *Gravelot*. He slays Hiram with the *Mallet*.

"As the brutal instincts do, when they attempt to create Order in the name of Violence, and Fear by crushing Intelligence."

"The branch of ACACIA on the grave of Hiram is like the Cross upon our altars.

"It is the *Sign* of knowledge surviving knowledge, the green branch that announces another spring."

[The acacia, or, as it is to be read, *akakia*, in the Greek ἀκακία, from ἀκή, a *point*, is that genus of trees to which belong that which yields the gum arabic, the mezquite, and the locust. It is the *satah* or *satam* wood of the Hebrew writings, שטה . . . שטם . . . *satah*, *satam*, used in the construction of the Tabernacle and the Temple, and therefore a Symbol of Holiness and Divine Truth. In the Greek, ἄκακος and ἀκακία mean freedom from evil, קדוש, *Holy*, *Holiness*, the TEMPLE, or HOLY HOUSE. It is, therefore, not the Symbol of Immortality alone, but of that life of innocence and purity for which the Faithful hope when they shall have been raised up to a new and spiritual existence.]

"When men have so troubled the order of nature, as the slayers of Hiram did, Providence intervenes to re-establish it ; as Solomon, symbol of the Infinite and Creative Wisdom, did to avenge the death of Hiram.

" He who assassinated with the Rule dies by the poniard.

" He who struck with the Lever or the Square will die under the axe of the law. This is the eternal sentence of the Regicides.

" He who completed the murder with the Mallet, falls a victim to the Force which he abused, and is strangled by the Lion.

" The Assassin by the Rule is denounced by the very Lamp that gave him light, and the Spring at which he drinks.

" That is to say, he is subjected to the *lex talionis*.

" The Assassin by the Square will be surprised when his vigilance is at fault, like a dog asleep, and he will be betrayed by his accomplices ; for Anarchy is the Mother of Treason.

" The Lion that devours the Assassin by the Mallet, is one of the forms of the Sphinx of Œdipus.

" And whosoever shall have conquered the Lion, will deserve to succeed to the dignity of Hiram.

" The body of Hiram, putrefied, shows that forms change, but the spirit remains.

" The stream which flowed near the first murderer, refers to the deluge which punished unnatural crimes.

" The Burning Bush and Rainbow, which cause the second Assassin to be discovered, represent Light and Life denouncing violences against Thought.

" In fine, the Lion vanquished represents the triumph of Spirit over Matter, and the definitive submission of Force to Reason.

" Since the beginning of the toil of the Spirit to build the

Temple of Unity, Hiram has been killed many times, and always raised again to life.

"He is ADONIS killed by the wild boar, OSIRIS assassinated by *Typhon.*

"He is PYTHAGORAS proscribed, ORPHEUS torn by the Bacchantes, HERMES, HORUS, MITHRAS, CAMA, ATYS, BALDER, MOSES abandoned in the caves of Mount Nebo, JESUS put to death by Judas, Caiaphas and Pilate.

"The true Masons, then, are those who persist in striving to build the Temple according to the plan of Hiram.

"Such is the grand and principal legend of Masonry. The rest are not less fine nor less profound, but we do not think it right that we should divulge their mysteries; though we have received initiation of God and our labors alone, we regard the secrets of High Masonry as our own. Having by our efforts attained a scientific degree which imposes silence on us, we hold ourselves more firmly bound by our convictions than by our oath. Science is a Nobility which obliges; and we will not be unworthy of the princely crown of the Rose Crosses. We, too, believe in the resurrection of Hiram.

"The Rites of Masonry are devoted to transmitting the remembrance of the legends of initiation, and preserving it among the Brethren.

"We shall, perhaps, be asked how, if Masonry is so sublime and so holy, it could have been proscribed and so often condemned by the Church?

"We have replied to this question in speaking of the schisms and profanations of Masonry.

"Masonry is the Gnosis; and the false Gnostics have caused the true to be condemned.

"What compels them to secrecy, is not fear of the Light: light is what they wish, seek for, and adore.

"They fear the profaners—that is to say, the false interpreters, the calumniators, the skeptics with their stupid laugh, the enemies of every creed and all morality.

"In our time, moreover, a great number of men who believe themselves Free Masons, are ignorant of the meaning of their Rites, and have lost the key of their Mysteries.

"They do not even any longer comprehend their symbolic pictures, and as little understand the hieroglyphical signs with which the hangings of their Lodges are decorated.

"These pictures and signs are the pages of the book of the absolute and universal knowledge.

"They can be read by the aid of the Kabalistic clues, and hide nothing from the Initiate who possesses the keys of interpretation of Solomon.

"Masonry has not only been profaned, but it has even served as a veil and pretext for the plottings of anarchy, by the secret influence of the avengers of Jacques de Molai, and the continuers of the schismatic work of the Temple.

"Instead of avenging the death of Hiram, his Assassins have been avenged.

"The Anarchists have retaken the Rule, the Square, and the Mallet, and written on them, 'LIBERTY, EQUALITY, FRATERNITY.'

"That is to say, Liberty for the covetous to plunder, Equality for the basest, and Fraternity to destroy.

"These are the men whom the Church has always condemned, and always will condemn."

These interpretations are ingenious, but not correct.

In the Hebrew, חרם, Khrm, meant 'devoted, consecrated,' devoted to the sacrifice as a victim. חור means 'white, an aperture, a window.' The name of the Artificer is, in Kings, Khirm; and in Chronicles, Khurm. Whether the second syllable is *am, ûm* or *ōm*, is uncertain.

Also, חי, khi, means 'life, living, alive:' אלהא־חיא, Aloha-Khia, 'the Living God.' And ראם, râm, meant 'was, or shall, be raised, elevated.'

The English Masonry was Christian (which means Trinitarian) from the beginning, and in it Hiram was the representative of Christ. In the Scottish Masonry he represented Jacques de Molaï, and Charles I. of England. But in it he became afterwards the representative of civil and religious liberty. Khur or kur, in Persian, means 'the Sun, Light :' and Hiram or Huram (*Khûrôm, ûm or ûm*), personifies moral, political and religious Truth. He is the Apostle of Truth, the Tribune of the People, the Reformer, the Defender of Free Thought.

Christ, preaching the equality of men before God, and making of those who followed him a Brotherhood, denouncing oppressors and hypocrites, scourging the money-changers out of the Temple, selecting his disciples among the poor of the Earth, became the type, in Free Masonry, of the Man of the People, endeavouring to enfranchise and elevate them.

To know whom his assassins personify, ask by what agencies such men have always disappeared from the earth.

ROYALTY fears the PATRIOT, and, as fear is always cruel, sends him to the scaffold. The PRIESTHOOD convicts the daring INQUIRER and philosophical THINKER, of Heresy or Contumacy, and professing to abhor the shedding of blood, delivers him to the secular arm to be murdered. The PEOPLE, slave of both the Crown and the Tiara, as a mob, or embodied as soldiery, executes with brutal violence the savage will of both.

At the Station of the Junior Warden, Hiram is stricken with the RULE, or twenty-four inch GAUGE, on the *throat.* At the Station of the Senior Warden, with the angle of the SQUARE, over the *heart :* and at the Station of the Master, with the SETTING-MAUL, on the *forehead.*

In the THROAT are the organs of speech : the HEART was for ages spoken of as the seat of the affections, and is so yet; and the FOREHEAD is the Seat of the Intellect.

What is meant by the three implements? Evidently they are symbolical. Men intending to extort a Secret, or take life if refused, would not arm themselves with rules and small squares. Webb and Cross, and the babblers of their school, who have never rightly interpreted a single Symbol, have not attempted to interpret these. Their business has been to more completely obscure the meaning of all the Symbols, by leading thinkers and thoughtless alike *away* from the truth, by trivial and worthless interpretations, whereby the Symbols have lost all value.

The clue to the meaning of the first of the three Symbols, the RULE, is, that in the Greek, a RULE, whether an implement, or a rule of conduct, or law, is *κᾰνών, canōn;* and the Law of the Church of Rome, derived from various sources, has always been called "The Canon Law."

The RULE, therefore, canōn, is an apt Symbol of the Church; and, in connection with the putting to death of Jesus of Nazareth, of the Jewish Church, represented by Annas and Caiaphas, the High Priests, who most urgently demanded and urged the People to demand the crucifixion of Christ, before Pilate and Herod, even inciting them, when Pilate desired to release him, to demand the release instead, of the thief, Barabbas.

The Jewish Priesthood at Jerusalem desired to silence Christ, being exasperated by his denunciations of their hypocrisy and vices: and therefore the Junior Warden, with the RULE, Symbol of the Pontifical and Sacerdotal Power, smote Hiram on the throat, where the organs of speech are.

Augustus Cæsar became the absolute Tyrant of Rome, not by usurping power, but by uniting in his own person all the great offices of the State, and so investing himself with all the powers of Government. Possessed of all Civil and Judicial Power, he also became possessor of all Religious Power, by becoming Pontifex Maximus; and all this accumulation of powers his Successors inherited.

The rigid, unbending Square of Steel, its two arms uniting to form the unyielding unity of the right angle, is an apt Symbol of the Imperial Power of Rome, union of all Civil and all Religious Power, a hard, harsh, unrelenting, merciless Despotism, its laws the edicts of an arbitrary will, and, whether just or unjust, executed without ruth or pity.

Wherefore, and because every Despotism, jealous, suspicious, and cruel, because suspicion and jealousy are cowardly, and always cruel, crushes without mercy or remorse the affections of the heart, upon mere suspicion sends the husband or father to Siberia, or to hard labour in mines, or to a dungeon for life, consigns to exile, imprisonment, or death, even the nearest blood-relations of the Tyrant, lest they should have partizans, and the disaffected should gather around them, and imperil the Tyrant's tenure of the throne, the Senior Warden smites Hiram with the Angle of the Square over the heart, the Seat of the Affections.

The Maul or Mallet, like the Club, a brutal weapon which crushes and defaces the image of God in Humanity, is a fit Symbol of the mob, blind and unreasoning, beating down and crushing with brute force whatever resists its mad rage, or has excited its insane suspicions. Utterly without reasoning, and hating cultivation and enlightenment, it looks upon the men of thought, the Statesmen and Scholars, and Thinkers, as its enemies, and like Jack Cade, considers knowledge a crime. Wherefore, at the Station of the Master, Hiram is stricken with the Setting-Maul upon the forehead, Seat of the Intellect, and falls stunned and crushed at the feet of the third Assassin.

Reason and Intellect have, in all ages, been found powerless, as they still are, to oppose a Military Despotism or organized Anarchy, in which alike the base and the brutal govern, and the good and the wise serve. The Revolutionary Tribunal, the Star Chamber, the Military Commission, Tribunals that sit sworn to condemn, and girded with bayonets, are the embodiments of this brute Force, and strike with its Club of Steel at the brain of Constitutional Freedom. It is the people that clamors for the blood of the Patriot; and the Soldiery is but the mob, organized and directed by a single will—an instrument, wielded like the Mace, blind and unreasoning as fate. In

the hand of Cyril it smites Hypatia, the Virgin enamored of
the old philosophy: in that of Marat it tears asunder the white
limbs of the Princess Lamballe, and offers the last indignities
to her palpitating flesh.   It howls after Rienzi as he treads the
road that leads to the scaffold: it digs up the bones of Cromwell at the will of an English Monarch, who becomes a pen-
sioner of the Throne of France.   It followed Christ with exe-
crations as he staggered under the crushing weight of the
Cross: it lauded Jeffries when he murdered under the forms of
English justice: it slaughtered the Grand Pensionary De Witt:
it yelled for the blood of Vergniaud, and would, if he had been
unsuccessful, have hounded Washington to the scaffold as a
Traitor.   It betrays and abandons its chiefs, and does not, like
Iscariot, repent, but obtains absolution for its own sins by as-
senting to the sacrifice of those whom it forced into rebellion
against the Throne, or the voluntary union of States.   There
is always a scape-goat devoted to Azazel, a sacrifice to expiate
the sins of the multitude: and God permits the people to be
base, in order to demonstrate the legitimacy of the despotisms
of the Cæsars, the Cromwells, and the Napoleons.

The _Crown_ itself is but a symbol, and Royalty is but the
most common type of tyranny.   The Kings of the mob are des-
pots also, and free States, like Athens or Sparta, subjugating
other free States, and animated by a vindictive revenge, strike
with the Rule at the throat, their anger and hatred taking the
form of law, and prohibiting the discussion of human or constitutional rights.   When, among Republics, Force decides
erroneously, as it always does, it becomes a crime, sometimes
called Treason, to be the advocate and defender of the Truth,
or even to re-state the facts of History.

The Mitre and Tiara also are but symbols, and the Pontifi-
cate but the most usual mode in which spiritual despotism
manifests itself.   Everywhere, and in every age, the Priest
covets temporal power; and in Republics, the pulpit becomes
the Tribune, and the dogmas and cruel angers of the Mountain

of Jacobinism become a part of the religion of Christ. The
Sanctuary goes back to the days of Moses and Joshua for its
precedents, and the Creed persecuted yesterday becomes the
persecutor of to-day. In all ages, the Priesthood, hater equally
of what it styles Heresy, and of true Liberty, makes Thought
and Opinions crimes. That murderously cruel Agency, the
Inquisition, was sanctified by being called "The Holy Office;"
as wars of religious persecution have been baptized by the
Church as "Holy Wars."

"He who assassinated by the Rule, dies by the poniard.
.  .  . He who struck with the Lever or the Square will die
under the axe of the Law. This is the eternal Sentence of the
Regicides."

Cæsar falls, pierced by the dagger of Brutus. The Tyrant
is deemed the enemy of the human race, and the Neros, Caligu-
las, Domitians, and Robespierres, like the Tarquins and the
Appii, are wild beasts whom it seems lawful to slay by any
means whatsoever. The victims of the Autocrat of the Tátars
and Cossacks in Poland, and the countless Exiles sent to die in
Siberia, are at last avenged by the Nihilist bomb that slays an
Emperor of Russia. But the truer Regicides than those who
so assassinate, or those who try and condemn the false and
faithless, or feeble King, the Charles or the Louis, are those
who assassinate the Kings of Thought, the Royalty of the Intellect. Justice is slow, but it at length overtakes the persecut-
ing Church, arraigns it before the great Tribunal of the Nations, and smites it with the axe of Justice, wherever it may
have been enthroned, and under whatsoever name it may have
usurped the prerogative of God. The blood of the Huguenot,
the Covenanter, and the Quaker, the Sicilian Vespers, and the
Eve of St. Bartholomew are always avenged at last by the justice of Omnipotence.

Tyranny is dethroned by the Intellect of which it consti-
tutes itself the patron, and by the burghers and the commons
to whom it grants privileges, that they may be bribed to sus-

tain it with moneys, and aid it in crushing the Nobles that endanger the power of the Crown : and the enemies of the Church —its Luthers and Wesleys—always spring from its own loins. Its own children turn upon it and rend it. It was the Monk of Einslieben that wounded the Romish Church unto death; and the Church of England has been, like Protestantism in Germany and New England, the nursing-mother of her deadliest foes.

But what if there should be other and profounder meanings than these, dangerous if known to the multitude, and only darkly hinted at by the Adepts?

What if KHUR-OM, Symbol of the LIGHT and representative of the SUN, and himself typified at his summer and winter solstices by Saint John the Baptist and Saint John the Evangelist, were also the Symbol of that Divine and Perfect TRUTH that dazzles the eyes of all except the Eagles and the Hawks, which in ancient Egypt were sacred to ATUM, AMUN-RA, and MENDES, the great Gods!

This Divine and perfect TRUTH, known only to the Hierophants and the Sages, and of which Herodotus, Hermes, and Plutarch speak in enigmas and by obscure hints, has often died and risen again from the dead. Wounded unto death by that literal interpretation of the holy writings that has been so fruitful of narrow and short-sighted creeds, it lived again and became immortal for the Initiates, when the Christ raised it, as he did Lazarus, its personification, from the tomb. The *Rule* and the *Square* are apt symbols of the rectangularity and stiff precision of that interpretation which makes a figurative Oriental book to have been written, as it were, in Geneva, or by an unimaginative Puritan or Presbyterian.

" *The Letter killeth ; but the Spirit vivifies.*" The Rule and Square of a stunted and pedantic verbal interpretation wounded this Divine Truth unto the death; and at last Orthodoxy always resorts to the Mace or Mallet of Force, with which the Priests slaughtered the sacrificial victim at the bloody altar which Israel borrowed from the worshippers of Baal and of Moloch, and whose horns dripping with gore revealed its origin. Thus read, the sacred oracles of all nations, intelligible to the Sages, are fruitful of idolatries among the vulgar. All the mythologies are but allegories accepted as the recitals of facts ; the Truth hidden under the veil of the Symbol remaining invisible within the Holy of Holies, where the Visible Presence dwells for the true Initiate between the cherubim.

# LEGENDA. II.

## The Aenigma of the Sphynx.

# THE

# ÆNIGMA OF THE SPHYNX.

---

It is in its *antique* Symbols and their occult meaning
that the true secrets of Freemasonry consist. These must
reveal its real nature and true purposes; and in these, also,
consists its superiority over all other Associations.

Not all its Symbols are ancient. Some were adopted from
the English and Scottish Craft of Stone-Masonry, when those
who created the order, somewhat before the beginning of the
eighteenth century, assumed the name of Free-Masons, by
which, in the old English statutes, those who worked in *free*
stone, as contradistinguished from those who worked in
*rough* stone, were known.* And some of the Symbols now

---

* The Statute of Labourers [25 Edw. III., *Stat.* 1] had this provision: *Item qe carpenters, masons, teglers, et auters coverours (or ov-rours) des mesons, ne preignent le jour pur
lour overeygne forsqe en manere come ils soloi-nt; cest assaver mestre carpenter iii d.
et autre ii d. mestre mason de franche piere iv. d. et autre mason iii d. et leur servantz
i d. ob.; teguler iii d. et son garceon i d. ob., &c.;* the translation whereof in the Statutes
at Large is, " Also that Carpenters, Masons, Tilers, and other workmen of Houses, shall
not take by the day for their work, but in manner as they were wont; that is to say, a
Master Carpenter three-pence, and another two-pence; a Master *Freemason* four-pence,
and other Masons three-pence, and their servants one penny half-penny; Tylers three-
pence, and their knaves one penny half-penny, &c.

The Statute 34 Edw. III., *Chap.* ix, entitled "The Statute of Labourers confirmed,
altered and enforced," provided that " the Carpenters and Masons take from henceforth
wages by the day, and not by the week nor in other marner; and that the Chief Masters
of Carpenters and Masons [*les chiefs mestres des Carpenters et Maceons*] take four-pence
by the day; and that all alliances and covines of Masons and Carpenters, and congre-
gations, chapters, ordinances, and oaths betwixt them made or to be made, shall be
from henceforth void and wholly annulled; so that every Mason and Carpenter, of
what condition soever he be, shall be compelled by his master to whom he serveth, to
do every work that to him pertaineth to do, either of *free stone* or of *rough stone*, [*ou de
fraunche p-re ou de grosse pere*]. And also every Carpenter in his degree."

And in the Statute 2 & 3 Edw. VI., *Chap.* xv., entitled " An act touching Victuallers used in the Blue Lodges of the United States are of still more recent manufacture; as, for example, Time combing out the ringlets of the Virgin's hair, and the two parallel lines with the Holy Bible resting upon them.

Freemasonry has been many different things, at different periods, and in the hands of different persons. It is not one and the same thing everywhere now. In some countries it is now a political association, its degrees having for its Initiates no philosophical signification whatever. In the United States, the Blue Degrees teach morality only, refuse to intermeddle with questions political or religious, and require only a belief in God, and, faintly, in the immortality of the soul; except so far as they declare the Holy Bible to be the rule and guide of man's conduct, and the inspired Word of God; which, if it were not evaded in practice, by the admission of Hebrews, would make the Masonry of the United States a strictly Christian Association. In the earlier part of the eighteenth century, Freemasonry was, for many of its Initiates, the teaching of the Hermetic philosophy. There are, we are told, six different Kadoshes, that which belongs to the Ancient and Accepted Scottish Rite being the veritable philosophical Kadosh: and so there have been, and still are, several Freemasonries, of which this Rite is the only true philosophical one.

It has been objected to us, that in our lectures we undervalue that which is absurdly called "Symbolic Masonry," as if any Masonry could be not symbolic.

It is quite true that we should not value it, if we saw nothing in the Symbols of the Blue Lodge beyond the imbecile

---

and Handicraftsmen," we find "the Craft, mystery or occupation of Victuallers" spoken of, and provision "that no person or persons shall at any time after the first day of April next coming, interrupt, deny, let, or obstruct any *Free Mason*, *Rough Mason*, Carpenter, Bricklayer, &c., to work in any of the said crafts."

And in the Statute 3 & 4 Edw. VI., *Chap.* xx., repealing a certain branch of the act last before mentioned, and reciting it, we find "the Artificers and Craftsmen of the arts, crafts, and mysteries aforesaid" spoken of, and "the *Free-men*, being artificers of the *crafts*, *arts*, and *mysteries* aforesaid."

pretences of interpretation of them contained in the ordinary sterile instruction which we owe to Webb and his predecessors. These misinterpretations are not so much guesses at the true meaning, as merely arbitrary and unwarranted explanations, invented with but a moderate degree of ingenuity, and no more authoritative or genuine than any others that an ingenious fancy might invent to-day. To pretend that they have been transmitted to us from antiquity is a mere fable. By the same process, an Egyptian hieroglyph might be made to mean anything.

To these pretended interpretations it is owing, and to those blind guides who look no further into Masonry, that intelligent men find so little to attract and interest them in Masonic Symbolism, and that much which is found in the degrees seems trivial and sometimes absurd.

Freemasonry must once have had other and very different purposes, and other and vastly more interesting and important objects, than those for which, in the United States and England, at least, it now exists. All of its symbols, that are not merely modern inventions, have a concealed meaning, which never appeared in the Liturgies or Rituals, these containing only hints cautiously given, and ideas easily misunderstood (and so intended to be) by all but the Adepts.

The legends of the different degrees, that of the third included, and those which purport to give historical accounts of the progress and transmission of Masonry during the Middle Age, and up to the year 1700, are told as if they contained statements of facts. So were the parables of Jesus of Nazareth, spoken by him to his disciples, and which they found hard to understand. We have not felt at liberty to discard them. But these legends are neither historical nor traditional; and in that respect it is true to say that Masonry has no real traditions, but only inventions. There is not the

slightest evidence that the legend of the third degree is true.
It is not historical, and it has not come to us by tradition.
It is allegorical ; and its signification is revealed by the name
of the Hero of the legend in its resemblance to HERMES.
The accounts given of the connection of the Masons with the
rebuilding of the Second Temple are simply allegorical, having
a meaning which you may hereafter come to know: and the
recitals of the career of the Perfect Elect have no foundation
in fact.   They are but allegorical and legendary.   We pre-
serve them, but we do not give you or the world  solemn as-
surances of their truth, or gravely pretend that they are historical or genuine traditions.

If the Initiate is permitted for a little while to think so, it
is because he may not prove worthy to receive the Light ;
and that, if he should prove treacherous or unworthy, he
should be able only to babble to the Profane of legends and
fables, signifying to them nothing, and with as little apparent
meaning or value as the seeming jargon of the Alchemists.
In times when it is unpopular or dangerous to teach the
truth, Wisdom sometimes wisely wears the mask of Folly,
and many of the grotesque fables of the old mythologies and
of the myths that came afterward to be regarded as history,
had a like origin.

But when it is gravely and persistently attempted to trans-
form mere follies and pretended traditions into historical
facts, to deny or doubt which is to be heretical or sceptical,
and these pretended facts of history are imposed upon a
whole Order and upon the world, and excite the derision and
contempt of men of learning, it is time to endeavor, from
the mass of historical falsehoods, to extricate the simple truth.
If the fabulous and the false were ever useful to Masonry, they
have ceased to be so now, and it is able to stand alone without
their support.

That the Freemasonry of the present day dates more, at the most, than a few years back of the year 1700, is as utterly unsustained by evidence or tradition entitled to respect as the pretences that it is in any way or degree the successor of or connected with the Dionysian architects or the German workers in stone, or the English or Scottish Freemasons of the fourteenth, fifteenth, and sixteenth centuries, or as the fables of the holding of a Grand Lodge at York, by the son of Athelstane, or of the existence of a Grand Lodge in that place before the year 1780, or of Encampments of Masonic Templars anywhere in England from time immemorial.

There is no evidence that there was any *revival* of Freemasonry in England in 1717, or that the Lodges and Societies of operative Stone Masons then *became* bodies having no connection whatever with the operative " Art, Craft, and Mystery." There was, on the contrary, then or not long before, the institution of a *new* Association, for purposes carefully concealed, and which, for a concealed reason, assumed the name of Freemasonry.

We think that the concealed reason for assuming that name was, that the Hebrew word *Amon* means both a Mason and faithful or loyal; and that the new associates called themselves Masons, because of this double meaning of the Hebrew word, and because the Initiates were anciently called The Faithful; and we also think that the new Association was first established in Scotland, by adherents of the House of Stuart, represented Charles I. by Hiram, and meant by the word *Mason*, one faithful and loyal to that House.

There are concealed meanings, also, beyond any question, in words and phrases where, as yet, such meanings are unsuspected; as there were in the name of the Master and Architect, in the two grips that fail and the one that succeeds, in the names of the assassins, in the Symbolic Temple, its erection, its destruction, and its rebuilding, and in the Triads of the Lodge and ceremonial. Such meanings have already been found in questions and answers ard phrases which had seemed meaningless or absurd, as in the "chalk, charcoal, and clay," and the clothing of "blue and gold" of the Master. The real meaning of the substitute for the Master's word is concealed with singular ingenuity; and in this and other cases, ignorance has, by its interpolations, superadded a second veil, more impenetrable than the first.

We do not mean that there are these concealed meanings in *all* the degrees of the Ancient and Accepted Scottish Rite. Some of them, like other and more modern degrees, never had any particular meaning or significance or purpose. The inventors of degrees were not always adepts.

It is not Blue Masonry itself that we undervalue. Nor do we undervalue its symbols and legends. We contemn only the untrue explanations of them. They are themselves full of interest to us, and are worthy to be the subjects of incessant study. It may be that we *over-estimate* them. For we think that many of the Symbols had their origin in the infancy and at the source of civilization, that their interpretations were for many centuries transmitted from one to another of the adepts, and that many have been lost in the long passage.

Of other portions of the Symbolism, not more than two centuries old. there were also, we think, concealed interpretations, indicating the political and religious doctrines and purposes of those who used the degrees, invented the new Symbols, and appropriated the old. If this is to *undervalue* the three degrees, words have lost their meaning.

It seems to us that Masonic students, seeking to learn the real meaning of the Symbols of the Blue Lodge, have adopted wrong methods, sought in the wrong direction for the keys of interpretation, looked over and beyond that which lay at their feet and close to them all around, into a distant darkness, lighted only by the delusive gleams of *ignes fatui*. We do not speak of the babblers who have merely followed the old track, repeated the old commonplaces, and incubated only on the mysterious texts; but of the few real students who have endeavored by real scholarship to interpret the obscure oracles and elucidate the symbols of the Lodge.

These have overlooked the obvious truth that the symbols of antiquity were not used to *reveal*, but to *conceal*, like the hieroglyphs, the idols, and the sacred language of the Brahmins: that each is an enigma to be solved, and not a lesson to be read; a hieroglyph to be deciphered, and not the letter of a vulgar alphabet, familiar to all. *The symbols of the wise have in all ages become the idols of the vulgar.* "What! is this the Builder?" seems to us as far from being a true interpretation, as "marrow in the bone." That which is so rendered, and the necessity of the presence of *three*, can be made to reveal, we think, a wholly different meaning.

We do not believe that the meaning of the Blue Degrees or their symbols, or of any other of the degrees, is to be learned by explorations among the rubbish of Egyptian antiquity. Some of the symbols are to be found there, and, older still, in the religious mysteries of other countries: but the explanations were never written, for any to read who chose. Like the oracles of the Gods, they were always covered with a veil, spoken of in enigmatical language, and false interpretations of them publicly given, to mislead those to whom it was not deemed wise to intrust them. This was done in all the mysteries, to the end that it might be known, after a time, who among the many had the intelligence, the zeal, and the eagerness for knowledge, that could enable them to divine or entitle them to receive, in a higher circle, the true explanations, know the mysterious secrets, and become possessed of the Holy doctrine.

We think that these secret meanings are always concealed
in one manner and upon one plan, the same as those by which
the Alchemists and Hermetic philosophers and Kabalists
concealed their meaning under the double veil of their jargon
and its pretended interpretation, the true signification being
only hinted at and perhaps never openly disclosed.  We think
that there is less that is really trivial in the ceremonial of the
Blue Degrees than appears upon its face; and that almost
everything has an occult significance, much of which is perhaps so completely lost, that it may never be discovered.
We doubt if we yet know the meaning of some of the simplest
things: and we are sure that very little is correctly explained
in the Blue Lodge, even the preparation of the Candidate,
and the relative positions of the Compasses and the Square in
the different degrees.

We know that the mysteries of Mithra were practised in
Rome even after Christianity became the State religion
of the Empire.   There is no reason to doubt that the succession of Initiates was continued until the times of the latest
Crusades, in Syria and Asia Minor.   It is known that the
Ismaelites had secret ceremonies of some kind, and they still
survive among the Druses.   Such institutions, in such a
country, do not die out.   The testimony given when Philip
and Clement crushed the order of the Temple, proved at least
the fact that the Knights had brought from the East some
ceremony of secret initiation that the Pope hated, and perhaps the King feared.   The knowledge of the rites and
symbols of these initiations, even if confined to a few, was
not likely to be wholly lost among the successors of the
Templars, who would, on the contrary, cling the more firmly
to it because they were persecuted.   The Roman de la Rose
is symbolical, and so in the highest degree is the Divina Com-
media of Dante.   The Rosicrucians and the Alchemists, all

of whom were anti-papal, and the Hermeticists, had some knowledge of the ancient Initiations. Of this there is evidence enough. Naturally we should not expect to find it openly avowed.

Maier says: "Like the Pythagoreans and Egyptians, the Rosicrucians exact vows of silence and secrecy. Ignorant men have treated the whole as a fiction; but this has arisen from the five years' probation to which they subject even well qualified servitors, before they are admitted to the higher mysteries; and within this period they are to learn how to govern their own tongues."

Michael Maier wrote a work especially dedicated to "that Order which has hitherto lain concealed, but is now made known by the report of the Fraternity, and their admirable and probable confession;" and he is said to have transplanted the Rosicrucianism of Andreä from Germany into England.

At all events, we know that early in the seventeenth century, many of the learned heads in England were occupied with theosophy, kabalism, and alchemy. Chief among these was Dr. Robert Fludd, who began to write in 1616, and died in 1637. He wrote the *Summum Bonum*, published in 1629, and an *Apology for the Rosicrucians*, published in 1617. He was intimate with Maier, while the latter was in England, and as the books published in Germany, relating to alchemy or other occult knowledge, were sent to England and speedily translated, he could easily have become acquainted with the three works of Andreä.

About 1633 the name of Rosicrucians was dropped in England, and that of *Sophoi*, Sages or Adepts, adopted. "We transmute," said Fludd, "the dead stones into living philosophical stones." Elias Ashmole, the antiquary, was one of this sect, who, as is well known, was received into a Lodge of Operative Masons. He, with William Lilly, Drs. Wharton

3

and Hewson, and others, established a Society which had some
meetings at Warrington, about 1646, before it was finally
settled in London.   Their purpose was to construct, in the
literal sense of the word, the House of Solomon on the Island
of Bensalem, in secret, and they clothed their purpose in
symbols.   Nicolaï of Berlin says that they first erected the
pillars of Hermes, from whose holy sentences Iamblichus
answered all the doubts of Porphyry.   Then they advanced,
by a ladder of seven steps, to a chequered pavement, and
were shown the symbols of the Creation or the work of five
days.   And, Nicolaï says, "to cover their secret and mysterious
meetings, they got admitted, in London, into the Masons'
Company, and held their meetings at the Masons' Hall, in
Masons' Alley, Basinghall-street, and as freemen of London
could take the name of Freemasons."

There would of course be no history or record of the origin of
the new Initiation.   There is none of the origin of the mysteries
or of any Ancient Order.   Their first beginnings are always
secret, and not intrusted to the treachery of written records.

It is certain that the Association or Order became suddenly
and at a bound, a different thing from that which it was
before, ceasing at once to be operative, and multiplying its
members with great rapidity among all classes of men.   It is
especially nonsensical to derive Masonry in its present form
from the Steinmetzen and Operative Masons, while admitting
that neither of these ever practised anything like the Master's
Degree, in which, it may be said, Blue Masonry wholly consists.   We know that the Degree had no existence until the
year 1723, perhaps a year or two later.   It would naturally
be confined to a few, at first, and kept a profound secret.

Made in this way, probably by Desaguliers and his associates, it is in one sense modern, much more so than the
Rose Croix; but in another it is of an unknown antiquity;

for it had the symbols and the symbolic ceremony, in its chief features, that were first used by the Hierophants in India, and afterward carried into Assyria, Egypt, Phœnicia, Persia, and Greece; and it has condensed, as it were, into these symbols, all the great and mysterious truths of the old Theosophy and Philosophy. It is, indeed, to those who can read its symbols aright, philosophy embodied in and taught by Symbols.

Surely this is not to undervalue the Masonry of the Blue Lodges, in all the Degrees of which the Ancient Symbols are found intermingled with modern ones, adopted and adapted to mislead all but the Sages and the Adepts. Thus viewed, Freemasonry is the heritage given to us by the remotest Past; the greatest, the oldest, the most venerable of all human institutions. Its so-called traditions are but Symbols and Enigmas that speak an intelligible language to the Adept, who knows that they are neither the recital of facts verified by history, nor actual occurrences whose memory is preserved by tradition.

The Apprentice is bound to secrecy and silence alone, and his manhood and courage are tested by the faint images of the old Initiations. The Fellow-craft is amused by the rudimentary instruction known to school-boys. Yet each is surrounded by the old and eloquent Symbols of the Orient, which the Ancient Isis holds out to them, while no word issues from her silent, stony lips. The sands of the desert cover all but the head of the mysterious Sphynx, and that, impassive as the pyramids themselves, utters no oracles. The Master Mason sees in the ceremonies Symbols still more significant, and in which the profoundest truths are hidden; but for explanations he hears but an idle babble of words, and, if he knew aught of the truth, would begin to understand the allegorical punishment of Tantalus. He became a Master, that he might obtain the *Master's* WORD, and with it travel into *foreign countries and earn a Master's wages.* But he is misled by a *Substitute* that has for him no meaning, although it indeed contains his reward if he but knew it. So far from finding his Masonry universal, he cannot demand assistance in danger anywhere except in his own country, and wherever the English language is spoken. He cannot gain admittance into a Lodge in Denmark, Norway, or Sweden, and hardly in Canada, if the law of the Order is enforced there. Verily he has *not* the *Master's* WORD, by which to travel into foreign countries and earn the wages of a Master.

We have heard, even to nausea, the assertion a thousand times repeated, that the Degrees of the Ancient and Accepted Rite are no *higher* than the Blue Degrees, and that they are no part of genuine Masonry. They *are* higher, nevertheless, because they are not conferred indiscriminately on all, nor intended to be popular; and because they illustrate and explain the Symbols of the Blue Lodge. And they are Masonic, if by Masonry we mean initiation into the mysteries. If we do not mean that, all *Masonry* is contained in the Apprentice's Degree.

If the Ancient and Accepted Scottish Rite, the Masonry of Heredom, the Rose Croix and the Holy House, commends itself to, and satisfies those who obtain its Degrees, that is enough. It is not its mission to teach others; and still less, to publish in books, with a view to money-making, those things which ought to be taught in the sanctuaries only. We need not lament if others are satisfied with the instruction of the Blue Lodge; and if we advance slowly, we at least do not have to complain, year after year, until the world wearies of it, that the doors of our sanctuaries swing too smoothly on their hinges, and that our initiates are multiplied with dangerous rapidity, through over-eagerness for numbers and for the fees for receptions.

Masonry claims to be an advance toward the Light. That Light is Truth. How far does Symbolic or Blue Masonry advance toward it?

None of the Truths of physical science are taught in either of the Blue Degrees. The letter G hangs in the east, and the Candidate is told that it is the initial of the word Geometry; and the names of the seven liberal arts and sciences as known to the ancients are repeated to him, with the names of the five Orders of Architecture. His whole Geometrical instruction consists in looking at the diagram of the forty-seventh Problem of Euclid, and receiving no explanation of it.

Other Truth than that of the physical sciences is Moral, Intellectual, Political, or Religious.

Blue Masonry utters a few of the commonest dicta of moral Truth, known and familiar to all men in all ages. It does no more. It limits itself to so much as is useful to bind together in a kind of Brotherhood the mass of a numerous Order. In the lesser mysteries no more was ever required. Its four Cardinal Virtues are Prudence, Fortitude, Temperance, and Justice. An Initiate of a secret Order must be prudent and cautious to reveal nothing to the Profane, to conceal the fact that he belongs to the Order, or perhaps that there is such an one. He must have fortitude to foil all attempts by force or torture to compel him to divulge these secrets; and also to be able to do efficiently what the Order may require of him. He must be temperate, for the drunken man divulges all secrets and becomes incapable to perform any duty well; and he must be just to his fellows, and not wrong one of them of the value of anything, or there can be no unity or harmony. There *must* be harmony among the workmen, because harmony is essential to the success of every Secret Association. The tenets of the Order are said to be Brotherly Love, Relief, and Truth. These are common to every Association. Used everywhere, the name of Brother amounts to little anywhere, since the time of Jacob and Esau.

Thus the morality of Masonry in these Degrees suffices for its purpose, and aims at no more. The Brethren are to meet on the level, to act, walk, and work by the plumb, and to part on the square. They are punctiliously to obey the law of just dealing and honest uprightness. Without these, there could be no bond of union to insure the success of the objects of the Order. *What that object is, they are never told. It was not meant that they should know it.*

We hear nothing of generosity, of self-sacrifice, of toleration. Hiram is not the Apostle of these. He leads no crusade against Error, Bigotry, Intolerance, Abuses, and Villainies. He is simply the type of the Initiate who dies rather than divulge the Secret Word of the Association. The Apprentice is bound to Secrecy only: the Fellow-craft, to obey his Superiors, and to run to and fro when they command, and not to wrong a fellow or cheat a Lodge. The Master is to keep a Master's Secret; to aid and assist a comrade; to respect the virtue of his relatives; not to speak ill of him, not to strike or wound him, except in self-defence. In all this we see, not a great system of morals, but only enforce-ment of the mutual offices of service and duty, of the members of a Secret Association to which it was dangerous to be-long, and whose object was not known to the mass of initi-ates.

Compare all the moral teachings of the Blue Degrees with, we will not say the Sermon on the Mount, but the Proverbs of Solomon, the teachings of Socrates, Confucius, Zarathustra, Seneca, or Mahomet; and one page of either will convince any intelligent man that the Masonry of the Level, Plumb, and Square is not a system of Morals, not even the handbook or primer of such a system. The Zendavesta, the Chinese

Books, and even the Koran, are, in their moral teachings, to Blue Masonry, like an oration of Cicero or an essay of Plato to the first utterances of a child.

Of political truth, nothing whatever is taught in the Blue Masonry of the English Rite. Nothing is heard in it of free government, the rights of the people, the rights of man, or of free thought, free conscience, and free speech. On the contrary, the Mason was to be submissive to the laws of Parliament, the supreme Legislature, which had changed the succession to the Throne, and to support the House of Hanover against the House of Stuart, not engaging in plots or conspiracies against the State. There is nothing in the Ritual to offend Pope or King, Inquisitor or Jesuit. All the Symbols that had originally and still have in the Scottish Rite, a political meaning, have been assiduously misinterpreted, until they teach no political Truth whatever.

The Masonry of the Higher Degrees teaches the great truth of Intellectual Science; but as to all these, even as to the rudiments and first principles, Blue Masonry is absolutely dumb. Its drama *seems* intended to teach the resurrection of the body; but it teaches nothing more. As the truths of politics, the great principles of human freedom, free government, free thought, and free conscience could not safely be proclaimed to the mass of Initiates as the cause to which by their association and by the oaths that insured secrecy and co-operation, they were to be devoted, so it was unnecessary, for the purpose of such union and co-operation, to teach the philosophical truth.

Of this, and of religious Truth, all that is taught is included in a single question and answer: "In whom do you put your trust?"—"In God." It was necessary that a Candidate should profess his belief in a Deity, since otherwise his oath would have no more binding force than a simple promise.

For the purposes of the Order, no more was necessary. Wherefore he is taught nothing as to the nature of the Deity or of himself, nor is any inquiry made in regard to his notions of either. That he believes in some sort of God who will punish perjury, is enough: and even if his God be but a monstrous image of himself, a mere hideous or grotesque idol of the imagination, Blue Masonry asks no more and teaches him nothing.

If, when the lesser mysteries were communicated to all men indiscriminately, any number of men who knew them only, had continually and confidently magnified these mysteries, proclaimed that they taught and revealed wonderful things, a complete system of morals and all known truth; and insisted that there were no other and higher mysteries; if by these bold and impudent assertions they had come to be looked upon as Hierophants by the mass of Initiates, and inventing silly interpretations of the Symbols over which they stumbled, had led their flocks far away from the truth and made them in love with the babblings of folly, the true Adepts would but have smiled to see the multitude misled, and have permitted their blind guides to strut to the end in their tinselled glories. For all this would no more have added value to the lesser mysteries, or have diminished the value of the greater ones, than the imprisonment of Galileo caused the sun to revolve round the stationary earth. Every man of high intelligence, Initiate of the Lesser Mysteries, but ignorant of the Greater, would still have known that the former were but preparatory, and that there must be some place in which their symbols were explained and their real purposes made known.

How can the intelligent Mason fail to see that the Blue Degrees are but preparatory, intended to enlist, and band and bind together the rank and file of the Masonic army, for purposes undisclosed to them? that they *are* the lesser mysteries,

in which the Symbols are used to conceal the truth? They
do see and feel and know this; and hence the resort to higher
degrees which, known nowhere else in the world, teach nothing at all, and have no object or purpose.

The books of Bro. Oliver and others like him, are wholly
made up of that which Blue Masonry does *not* teach: and it
is a singular absurdity that a Rite should be valued and
lauded, not for what it *does* teach and disclose, but for what
the Initiate can only learn from books as open to be read by
the Profane as by himself. And it is a greater absurdity, if
that is possible, that nearly the whole of the immense mass
that has thus been written has little or no real connection with
Blue Masonry, and might with quite as much propriety have
been written upon any other text.

Of course nothing is to be done with those who accept
literally the legend of Hiram and of the building and rebuilding the Temple. In the Mysteries, those who misunderstood the Symbols and allegories were left to remain in the
complacency of their ignorance.

The existence of the Scottish Freemasonry, before 1717,
was not publicly known; for its purposes were, by the laws
of England and Scotland, treasonable. It was carried to
France by the adherents of the Pretender, and there used for
the same purpose, to unite the adherents of the House of
Stuart, and enable them to act in concert with those who,
during the reign of Anne and George I., were plotting to
restore the Stuart dynasty. There, also, it was connected
with the higher degrees, already existing, or from time to
time invented, in France. That the English Freemasonry,
established at the moment of the death of Anne, was the
creation of the adherents of the House of Hanover, is suf-
ficiently evident from the pledge of its Masters, that they
would obey the will of the Supreme Legislature, that is, of

the English Parliament which had changed the succession to the crown; for this promise was never exacted by the Scottish Freemasonry. And it also offers the only rational explanation of the rapid increase of the new association and of the existence of fifty or more Lodges in London in a few years.

The Symbols of Antiquity and a Ceremonial resembling that of the Mysteries, were perhaps used, at first, to conceal the true purposes of the Organization; and the certain destruction that would be caused by betrayal, while the aim of the Order was to overthrow the Government, accounts for the penalties of the obligations.

When there was no longer hope of the restoration of the Stuarts, the higher Degrees, which had become a part of the system of Scottish Freemasonry, were carried to England by the adherents of Laurence Dermott, of whose politics we know nothing; and with the annihilation of that hope the purposes of that Freemasonry changed. Becoming connected with some, and giving birth to others, of the higher Degrees, the system became philosophical and of course anti-papal, because Rome was the enemy of both Science and Philosophy. The English Masonry stood still. Suspicious of the higher Degrees, it refused to recognize them as Masonic, or to form any connection with them, or with the Royal Arch of Dermott, framed from the Royal Arch of Enoch. It changed its lectures and formulas, again and again; but it never had any especial object, after the struggle of the adherents of the Stuarts had ended. The Scottish Freemasonry, on the contrary, engaged in its long controversy with Royal and Pontifical Despotism, and became the apostle of Free Thought, Free Speech, and Free Conscience.

We do not demand your assent to these conclusions. We state them here, to lead you to reflect and study, that you may decide for yourself. All that we positively assert is, that

so far from containing in themselves all Freemasonry, the
Blue Degrees, especially in England and the United States,
only conceal the Light from the Initiates, were at the beginning only a means of organization, and are now only prelim-
inary and rudimental.   The Degree of Perfection is so called
because it *completes* and *perfects* the Third Degree.


THE END.

www.ingramcontent.com/pod-product-compliance
Lightning Source LLC
Chambersburg PA
CBHW030911260626
47169CB00008B/2798